Snow Surprise

Lisa Campbell Ernst

Green Light Readers
Harcourt, Inc.
Orlando Austin New York
San Diego London

"Surprise! Look at the snow, Joan!"
yelled her little brother, Ben.

Joan looked out.
The snow was so pretty!
Sport barked.

"I saw the snow first!
I saw the snow first!"
Ben sang.

Joan ran for her coat. "I'll show you
a snow surprise," she called to Ben.
Joan loaded her pockets with
all sorts of things.

"Don't look!" she said.
Then she ran out with Sport.

It was cold! Frost was on the porch.
Joan jumped off and landed in the snow.

Sport ran and jumped in the snow, too.
He nipped at the snow floating in the air.

"Come with me, Sport!" Joan called.

Joan packed snow into
a small ball. Then she
started rolling the ball.

"It's growing!" Joan yelled.

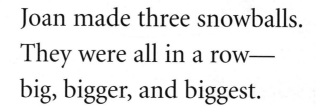

Joan made three snowballs.
They were all in a row—
big, bigger, and biggest.

Joan stacked the snowballs
to make her snow surprise.
She put one on top of
the other.

She patted on more snow to fill in the gaps. Sport barked at the crows and other birds.

At last, Joan added the
things from her pockets.
She had apples, nuts, yellow
corn, crusts of toast, and more.

Sport got sticks. Joan used
them to make arms. She put food
for the birds in bowls. Then she
loaned her own hat and scarf
to the snow surprise.

"Our snow surprise is perfect," Joan said to Sport. She ran in to get Ben.

Out in the yard, the birds saw
corn and toast. The animals
smelled nuts and apples.

What did Sport smell?
He smelled trouble!

In a flash, there *was* trouble. The birds snatched the food. The animals munched. It was a mad dash for the snacks!

Sport jumped at them all.
The snow surprise tipped.
Then it fell over with a *THUD*!

Joan led Ben out to show him the surprise. She gasped. It was not there!

"Oh no," Joan groaned.

Ben clapped his hands. "A mouse!" he sang.
"It's a snow mouse!"

Joan looked again. It *was* a mouse.

"Surprise!" she said.

What Do You Think?

Why do you think the author wrote this story?

What are the steps for making Joan's snow surprise?

Do you think the animals are happy that Joan is making a snow surprise? Why or why not?

Think about the ending. What do you think Joan and Ben will do next?

Write about something you made to surprise someone, or about a time someone surprised you.

Meet the Author-Illustrator

Lisa Campbell Ernst

Lisa Campbell Ernst grew up in a family that loved books and sharing stories. So, she would draw pictures and make up stories about the animals in her neighborhood. "I still love drawing animals!" she says. "I watched my friend's dogs Fred and Elmo playing outside. I watched the wildlife in my backyard for the other animals, and my daughter, Allison, to draw Joan."

Requests for permission to make copies of any part of the work should be submitted
online at www.harcourt.com/contact or mailed to the following address:
Permissions Department, Houghton Mifflin Harcourt Publishing Company,
6277 Sea Harbor Drive, Orlando, Florida 32887-6777.

www.HarcourtBooks.com

First Green Light Readers edition 2008

Green Light Readers and its logo are trademarks of Harcourt, Inc.,
registered in the United States of America and/or other jurisdictions.

Library of Congress Cataloging-in-Publication Data
Ernst, Lisa Campbell.
Snow surprise/Lisa Campbell Ernst.
p. cm.
Summary: Joan makes a surprise for her little brother,
Ben, but in the end, she is the one who is surprised.
[1. Snowmen—Fiction. 2. Brothers and sisters—Fiction. 3. Surprise—Fiction.] I. Title.
PZ7.E7323Sno 2008
[E]—dc22 2007042343
ISBN 978-0-15-206553-9
ISBN 978-0-15-206559-1 (pb)

C E G H F D B
C E G H F D B (pb)

Ages 5–7
Grade: 1
Guided Reading Level: F
Reading Recovery Level: 10

Green Light Readers
For the reader who's ready to GO!

"A must-have for any family with a beginning reader."—*Boston Sunday Herald*

"You can't go wrong with adding several copies of these terrific books to your beginning-to-read collection."—*School Library Journal*

"A winner for the beginner."—*Booklist*

Five Tips to Help Your Child Become a Great Reader

1. Get involved. Reading aloud to and with your child is just as important as encouraging your child to read independently.

2. Be curious. Ask questions about what your child is reading.

3. Make reading fun. Allow your child to pick books on subjects that interest her or him.

4. Words are everywhere—not just in books. Practice reading signs, packages, and cereal boxes with your child.

5. Set a good example. Make sure your child sees YOU reading.

Why Green Light Readers Is the Best Series for Your New Reader

• Created exclusively for beginning readers by some of the biggest and brightest names in children's books

• Reinforces the reading skills your child is learning in school

• Encourages children to read—and finish—books by themselves

• Offers extra enrichment through fun, age-appropriate activities unique to each story

• Incorporates characteristics of the Reading Recovery program used by educators

• Developed with Harcourt School Publishers and credentialed educational consultants